ORLAND PARK PUBLIC LIBRARY
14921 Ravinia Avenue
Orland Park, Illinois 60462
708-428-5100

HUDSON
THE
HIPPO

A TALE OF SELF-CONTROL

Published in 2011 by Windmill Books, LLC
303 Park Avenue South, Suite # 1280, New York, NY 10010-3657

Adaptations to North American Edition © 2011 Windmill Books
Copyright © Diverta Ltd 2009

CREDITS:
Text by Felicia Law
Illustrated by Lesley Danson

Library of Congress Cataloging-in-Publication Data

Law, Felicia.
 Hudson the hippo : a tale of self-control / by Felicia Law ; illustrated by Lesley Danson.
– North American ed.
    p. cm. – (Animal fair values)
 ISBN 978-1-60754-904-8 (lib. bdg.) – ISBN 978-1-60754-913-0 (pbk.) – ISBN 978-1-
60754-914-7 (6-pack)
[1. Hippopotamus–Fiction. 2. Self-control–Fiction.] I. Danson, Lesley, ill. II. Title.
PZ7.L41835Hud 2011
[E]–dc22
                                      2009053143

Manufactured in the United States of America

For more great fiction and nonfiction, go to www.windmillbooks.com.

CPSIA Compliance Information: Batch #BW2011WM: For further information contact Windmill Books, New York, New York at 1-866-478-0556.

HUDSON
THE
HIPPO

A TALE OF SELF-CONTROL

FELICIA LAW

ILLUSTRATED BY LESLEY DANSON

WINDMILL
BOOKS

Hudson woke up in a bad mood. This was not unusual. He often woke up in a bad mood.

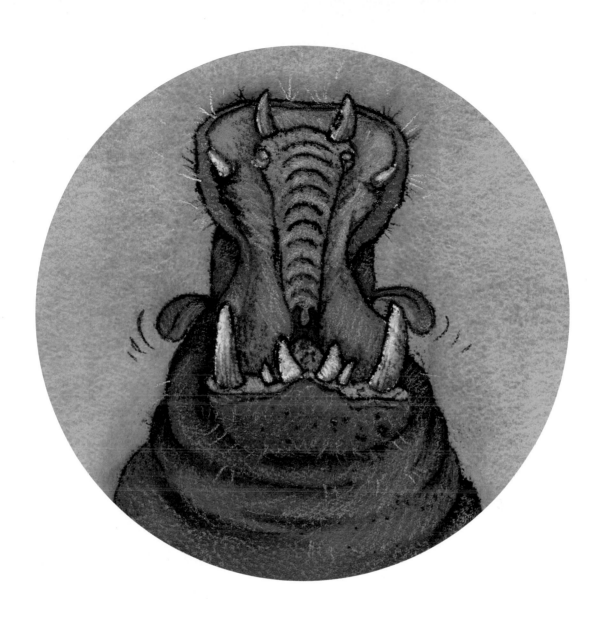

But today he felt like he couldn't
control himself!

There was no reason for his bad mood. The night before, Hudson had heaved himself out of the lake. As the Sun set, he went out to find his dinner.

6

He was a huge animal and he had a huge appetite. Sometimes he walked for hours, through most of the night, looking for grass to chew.

Then, back at the lake with a full
stomach, Hudson had sunk below the
surface of the water to sleep.

From time to time, his big, sleeping body
had floated to the surface without him
doing anything.

He came up for air, then sank down again,

Up and down, up and down . . .

...all night long.

But today, Hudson felt like the only thing that would make him feel better was if everyone else was in a bad mood, too.

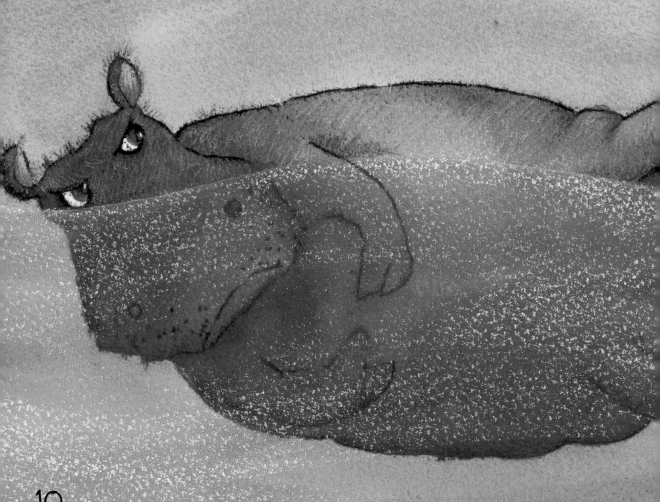

He gave an angry grunt and knocked his younger brother over on purpose.

Bump! Bump!

And that made Hudson feel a lot better!

Then he knocked his brother over again! Hudson was really out of control!

Bump!

Bump!

But Hudson's brother wasn't in a bad mood like Hudson. He knew how to control himself.

"Hi Hudson!" he said. "Do you want to play wrestling? What fun!"

"Of course I don't want to PLAY!" snorted Hudson.

Hudson was still angry. He looked around for someone else he could grunt at and bump.

There were lots of other young hippos around. Many were resting in the middle of the lake. Only their eyes, ears, and noses poked above the surface.

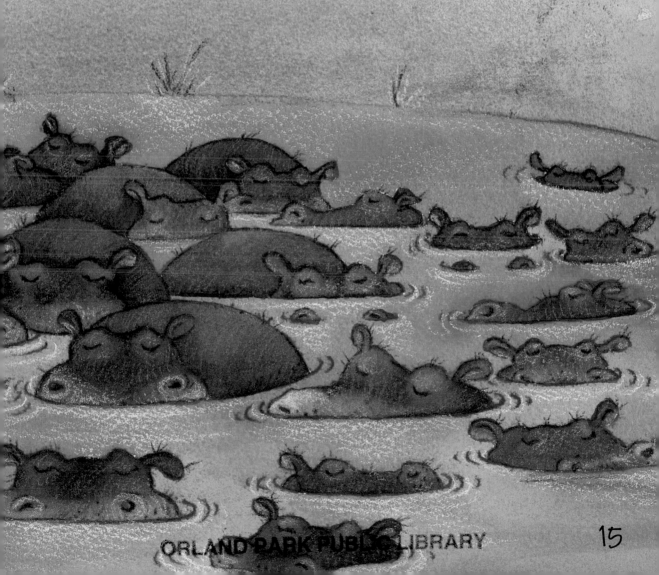

15

Splash!

Hudson frowned at them. They were having a good time. He'd put a stop to that! With a mighty leap, he threw himself into the deepest part of the lake, sending a great splash of muddy water over the herd.

Splash!

But the other hippos weren't
out of control like Hudson.

"Hey," they called. "Do you want to play?
We can splash each other! What fun!"

"Of course I don't want to PLAY!"
snorted Hudson.

17

"What a terrible temper you have, Hudson," they grunted. "You need to learn to control it."

Poor Hudson! He wanted everyone to be in a bad mood.

But the Sun was shining...

birds were singing in
the trees,

a family of monkeys
was playing tag,

and it seemed no one wanted
to be in a bad mood.

19

Then Hudson saw a crocodile with sharp teeth. The crocodile looked mean enough to be in a bad mood like Hudson. So Hudson bit his tail just to be sure.

Nip! Nip!

But the crocodile wasn't feeling nearly as mean as he looked, and he wasn't in a bad mood like Hudson.

"Hey," he snapped. "Do you want to play with me? We can pretend to bite each other!"

"Of course I don't want to PLAY!" snorted Hudson.

The tall cranes didn't look mean at all. But Hudson was so angry by now, he wanted to kick someone. So he marched right up to the flock,

and kicked.

Kick!

Kick!

The cranes had long legs and they could kick, too.

"Hey," they called. "Do you want to play? Let's kick! What fun!"

"Of course I don't want to PLAY!" snorted Hudson.

By now Hudson was so mad that he didn't notice the rhino with the white horn until he'd almost bumped into it.

Unlike Hudson, rhinos are mostly peaceful creatures. But they do get angry when another animal gets too close.

"Hey!" growled the rhino. "Look where you're going! What's your problem, anyway?"

"I warn you," said Hudson, "I'm in a really bad mood!"

"You're in a bad mood?" asked the rhino.
"Well, if you want to fight, let's fight!"
The rhino lowered its wrinkled snout and
pricked up its ears.

It looked ready to charge at Hudson!

Hudson looked at the rhino's horn, at the hump on its back, at the bristles on its tail, and at the dust rising from its feet...

Did he really want to find out what happened when someone else got mad and didn't have self-control?

Hudson looked back at the cranes, still kicking their legs in a wild dance...

at the crocodile snapping at its own tail...

and at the hippos splashing in the cool water.

He looked at the Sun and the trees
and the tall grass...

He took a deep breath and felt calm.
He felt in control of his feelings.

"Maybe tomorrow," Hudson said to the rhino in a happy voice. He turned his back on the surprised animal, and he went back to play with his friends at the lake.

Maybe if he had more self-control, he could have more fun!

LEARN MORE

ABOUT THE HIPPO

Hudson is a pretend hippo. Here are some facts about real hippos.

- "Hippo" is short for "hippopotamus."
- The hippo lives in the southern half of Africa.
- Hippos live in rivers and lakes. They spend half their time in the water and half out.
- A hippo needs to spend a lot of time in water to keep its skin cool and moist.
- Hippos leave the water at sunset to feed on grass. Sometimes they must walk many miles (km) to find food.

ABOUT SELF-CONTROL

Hudson the Hippo is a story about learning to control angry feelings. It follows the day of a young hippo who wakes up in a bad mood and who tries to make everyone else feel bad, too. In the end, when Hudson learns to control his feelings, he has a much nicer day with his friends.

It's okay to feel sad or angry or to want to be left alone, but picking fights with others isn't a good way to deal with those feelings. It doesn't help others to understand what you are feeling. Self-control means not taking your bad moods out on others and learning to explain your feelings in words.

Glossary

Appetite (A-pih-tyt) A desire for food.

Charge (CHARJ) To run at someone in an attack.

Grunt (GRUNT) To make a short, deep sound.

Temper (TEM-pur) Angry mood.

Index

FOR MORE INFORMATION

Books

Feldhake, Glenn. *Hippos: Natural History & Conservation.* Osceola, WI: Voyageur Press, 2005.
Iozzia, Victoria. *I'm Lu the Hippopotamus.* Bloomington, IN: Xlibris Corporation, 2008.

Web Sites

For Web resources related to the subject of this book, go to:
www.windmillbooks.com/weblinks and select this book's title.